A PET

MW00942613

HAMSTIGATOR

The Super Coolest Pet Ever. Possibly.

Michael Andrew Fox

Illustrated by Ed Shems

For more information, visit us online at:
www.petimalsbooks.com

Like us on Facebook at:
www.facebook.com/petimals

Praise for the first Petimals book, DOGOPOTAMUS:

"This fun story will provide the young reader a delightful experience. Parents will love the opportunity to talk about other possibilities. This book provides an enjoyable read and will spark some creative, divergent thinking in the young reader."

Cheryl J.

"The story is adorable. My grandchildren loved it. They could relate to the children and their fantasy. My grandson has gone back to read it again."

Barbara S.

"Well written, fun and enjoyable read. Our grandchildren loved the story. We all look forward to the next Petimals Book."

Nancy M.

"The story is well written from inside the imaginative mind of a curious, young boy. His excitement along with his easily distracted inner monologue kept me smiling, while the illustrations kept me chuckling at every page turn."

Jarrod L.

"What a wonderful story! Dogopotamus allows the imagination to take over. I laughed out loud throughout the entire book and the illustrations were perfect! I bought 4 books so far and definitely plan to buy more."

Ashleigh M.

Ed Shems

For my son, Leo, who loves to watch the illustrations grow.

A PETiMALs Book

HAMSTIGATOR
The Super coolest Pet Ever. Possibly.

Michael Andrew fox
Illustrated by Ed Shems

CONTENTS

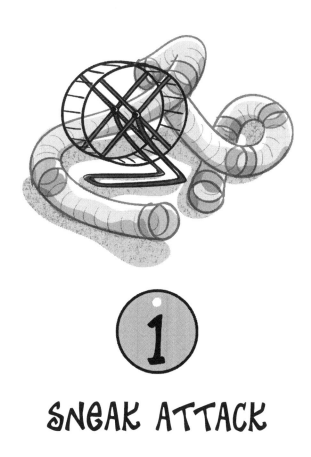

1

SNEAK ATTACK

The first rays of morning sunlight come

through my bedroom window. I watch a beam

of yellow slowly creep across the wall next to

my bed. I've been awake for a while, staring at the ceiling, just waiting to get up and go downstairs for breakfast. The breakfast table is where I do my best work. It's my office. My sharpest negotiating tactics all take place between the hours of 6:30 and 7:45 a.m. Instead of fancy chairs, coffee, and three-piece suits, my boardroom consists of a round, wood table, fruity cereal, and sharky pajamas. Shirt optional.

My target: adults over the age of 30 who, somehow in their advanced age, have lost the ability to think clearly before 7 o'clock.

Perfect situation for me. Anytime I want something, need something, or have to bargain for something, this is THE time to do it. Unfortunately, my biggest roadblock is my older brother, Zack. Nobody kills a perfectly executed plan like he does. He's equal parts boring, lame, and annoying. Zack thinks all my ideas are stupid, and instead of just sitting there minding his own business, he has to make a face or a comment, or otherwise say something that somehow snaps our groggy parents out of their morning fog. No breakfast table board meeting ever goes well when he's around.

That's why I've been staring at the ceiling above my bed for the past hour. Today's negotiation is particularly important. I'm ready, again, to ask for a pet. I'm not talking about just any pet. This one is going to be special, and it will require special bargaining tactics. I need total concentration and no distractions. Dad isn't around this morning because he's traveling for work. Zack should still be asleep, so it'll just be Mom and me. Mano a Momo.

I get up and put a matching pajama shirt on today. You're always taken more seriously with a shirt on. Even though it's nearly summer and I don't sleep with one when it gets hot, I feel like I should be slightly more formal this morning. I could put on slippers, or actually get dressed for school, but that would be a dead giveaway that I was up to something. I open my door as quietly as I can and slowly walk down the hallway towards the stairs.

There is no way to get downstairs without having to pass by my brother's room. What a pain! The floors are made of hardwood, and it seems each step I take creates a symphony of cracks and pops. What's up with floors not making noise any other time of the day, but early in the morning they sound like I'm stepping on bubble wrap? I hate hardwood floors!

As quietly as I can, I make my way past Zack's door. As I sneak by, I hear the faintest sound of scurrying. One of Zack's turtles, I'm sure. Not exactly the greatest lookout pet. Lame.

I head downstairs, slowly making my way through the first floor hallway and into the kitchen. I sit at the table and wait. The old clock on the wall reads 6:15 a.m. A little early, but any minute now Mom will come into the kitchen and my workday will begin.

It seems like an eternity. I swear I can hear that old clock on the wall tick-tick-ticking away. Finally, at 6:25 a.m. Mom emerges from her bedroom. With her eyes half-closed, she stumbles into the kitchen. I adjust myself in the chair and scoot in a little closer to the table, trying to make it look like I had just sat down.

"Morning Coby," Mom says, wiping her eyes with the back of her hands. "You're up early today."

"Morning Mom. Yeah, I just got up." Wink, wink.

8

She stretches out her arms, and in the middle of a yawn says, "A-a-a-r-e y-y-o-o-u r-e-e-a-a-dy for breakfast? I can make you some cereal."

Perfect! She's barely awake.

"Sure," I say, rolling my eyes. Cereal again? Seriously? Is there nothing else in this house for breakfast?

Mom moves in slow motion as she tries to locate all the super complicated ingredients that make up a bowl of cereal. She goes from the pantry to the fridge, back to the pantry, over to the cupboard, back to the fridge, pulls

out 3 drawers before she finds a spoon, back

to the pantry and finally over to the kitchen

table. It's like watching a Ping-Pong game at

half speed.

I'm pretty sure she put the milk back in the

cupboard and the box of cereal back in the

fridge. This is going to be easier than I thought.

She sits down at the table to catch her breath. I take one spoonful of sugary cereal for a burst of energy and decide there's no time like the present. Here goes nothing...

"Mom, I would REALLY like to have my own pet," I say, easing her into the conversation.

"What exactly did you have in mind this time, Coby?" she asks as another yawn comes out.

This time? Obviously she hasn't forgotten about last time. Dogopotamus was a great idea on paper, but he was just too big. I need something cool, but compact. The perfect combination of exciting and fun, but medium-sized and manageable. And, I think I've found it!

"I have the perfect idea, Mom," I say as I sit up in my chair and lean forward into my pitch position.

I didn't think you could stop a yawn midway through, but Mom seems to manage it. She furrows her eyebrows, squints at me in the morning light and waits.

"Mom...I would like to have...as my very own pet...a medium sized...alligator."

The word "Alligator" just hangs there between us like a thought bubble in comic strips. I can hear my own heartbeat as the whole house goes silent. Even the clock on the wall stops ticking.

Mom stares at me, I stare at Mom, Zack rolls over in bed, and somewhere in the house one of the North American Box Turtles flips over onto its shell.

2

SEWER CREATURES

"Coby," she says, finally breaking the silence. "You CANNOT have an alligator as a pet!"

"Come on, Mom" I say, trying to act surprised, even though I knew she was going to say that.

Here comes my pitch.

"Mom, Brent from across the street told me a story about these creatures that live in the sewers underground," I said. "They swim inside the pipes and can come in the house through the toilets. Pretty scary, huh?"

She doesn't say anything. She just blinks once and keeps staring at me with a confused look on her face. I keep going.

"I was thinking we could use a little protection. Alligators aren't that big. It can hang out in the backyard. We can dig a hole and fill it with water so he can swim. He can scare those sewer creatures away. And, maybe he'll also scare away those rabbits that you always complain about. Stop them from eating your garden in the backyard. It would be so cool."

I was starting to feel like my arguments weren't strong enough, but between the sewer creatures and the rabbits, she had to consider it, right?

Mom keeps staring at me as if a sewer creature might crawl out of my ear. Finally, she snaps out of her trance.

"Coby, there is NO way you can have an alligator," she says. "For one thing, sewer creatures don't exist. Plus, you can't keep an alligator in the house. They have huge teeth, they're too scary and too dangerous."

Rats! I guess Mom isn't as tired as I thought. Next time I'll try waking her up in the middle of the night.

Mom gets up and leaves the room just as Zack comes wandering into the kitchen. He doesn't look any more awake than Mom did when she first got out of bed. Maybe I can convince him.

"Hey Zack, yesterday at school, Brent told me a story about these creatures that live in the sewers underground. They swim inside the pipes and come in the house through the toilets. Pretty scary, huh?"

Zack doesn't say anything as he sits down at the table. His eyes are half shut.

"I'm just thinking we could use some protection," I add. "You know, in case something gets into the house. I was just talking to Mom about me getting a new pet and she said maybe I could get an alligator."

Zack yawns, looks at me and squints his eyes as if the sun is shooting into them. He finally snaps out of his trance and says, "Nice try Coby, but I don't think so. There aren't any creatures that live in the sewers and pop up out of the toilets. You AND Brent are crazy."

Double rats! Is this whole family full of morning people?

Mom comes back into the kitchen. She sits down next to me and begins to rub my arm in a comforting way. I can tell she's considering my pet request.

"Why don't you start with something small and simple, Coby," she says. "Like a goldfish."

"Or, maybe a hamster."

Ugh.   Next time I'm talking to Dad first.

This is getting me nowhere.

3

THE DRAWING BOARD

I try to put the whole pet issue out of my mind for the day, but after dinner I decide to spend some time in my bedroom and figure out what went wrong. Mom suggested a hamster, but they're not cool at all. Just little furry creatures that crawl through tubes, run on plastic wheels, and otherwise don't do much of anything. Maybe if they could swim, or had big teeth or something, then they'd be more interesting. I look over at my drawing of Dogopotamus pinned up over my bed. He would have been SO cool!

Just then it hits me. I can make a hamster a lot more interesting if I make some modifications. Hamsters have cute bodies but they're not exciting enough. What if I take all the things I love about alligators and some of the things I like about hamsters and create a new pet? I grab a piece of paper from the bottom drawer and a black crayon from a cup on my desk. Hamsters are kinda cute. I like the furry body, so let's start there. I draw a round, chubby body and color in some fur. I don't like the hamster's mouth or nose, so let's use the alligator's. I add a long alligator head with big teeth. Let's put some fur on top of its head, like the hamster.

The more I draw, the more I can see my new creature starting to take shape on the paper.

Hamsters are too chubby, so let's make my new pet longer and leaner. I grab an eraser and use it to thin out the body. I like alligator tails, so let's add that too. Alligators don't have ears, so we can keep the hamster's. I finish drawing a spiny tail, and then add some little round ears on top of its head.

My excitement grows as the drawing on the page begins to come together. This could turn out to be a VERY cool pet. Next come the feet. A hamster has short, stumpy arms and legs, but so does an alligator. Let's go with the alligator's. I draw in four short legs and add some sharp claws. I take one last look at the whole creature and make a few last minute adjustments.

"Narrow the eyes a bit, make the tail a little longer, and the feet a little wider," I say out loud to myself. "Add some stripes, give him a cool collar and there you have it!"

I push back from the desk and soak in what I have just created. Another work of art that can only be described as the coolest creature ever! Behold, the very first of its kind. The one…the only…Hamstigator!

I take the drawing of my new pet, walk it over to my bed and with 4 pushpins hang it on the wall, right next to Dogopotamus. I lay down, hands behind my head, and imagine the possibilities.

BALL OF FUN

I imagine Hamstigator sitting in his cage, waiting for me every morning when I get up.

"Hey, Hamstigator," I say, as I get out of bed with a yawn. "How are you today?"

Hamstigator yawns too, flashing a mouthful of sharp teeth. He wanders over to the side of his glass cage as if to say, "Morning, Coby.

Let's play!"

I slowly reach into the cage and pick up my

new pet. I make sure to grab him across his

back, just behind his ears. Those teeth are

pretty intimidating, even though he never

bites me. He's not too heavy and he's only about a foot long. The perfect size for a pet, easy to play with and not so big that he's going to destroy things.

"What would you like to do, buddy?" I ask. "How about taking a spin in your plastic ball?"

Hamstigator wags his spiny, green tail with excitement. I grab the oversized clear plastic ball I bought for him and split it in half like an egg. I stuff Hamstigator into one side, then close the other half around him, putting the ball back together. Hamstigator immediately starts pumping his little legs, making the ball roll across my room. He races around the room, bumps into a wall, changes directions, and then bumps into another wall. Each time it makes a loud thud. He can definitely put some power into that rolling ball!

I let him cruise around in his ball for a while until he slows down and starts to look tired. I crack open the ball and drop him back into his cage.

His cage is awesome. It's a huge glass tank filled with wood chips. There is a little plastic pool at one end, a giant hamster wheel in the middle, and a maze of multi-colored tubes running around the top. The tubes are just big enough for Hamstigator to fit through. They connect to each other and snake in every direction around the top of his cage.

Once I drop him into the tank, he immediately climbs up into the tubes and starts crawling around. He runs through the tubes until he hits a fork in the road, then he chooses a side and keeps running. He does it for hours! He finally comes out, walks over to his pool and slides under the water. He floats to the top, and all that's showing is his head, hamster ears and eyes. He looks just like an alligator floating along a river looking for food.

Food! Hamstigator needs food. What do Hamstigators eat? What do alligators eat? I have NO idea. Probably fish and birds, but I don't have anything like that here. I'm not even sure what hamsters eat…but I know who I can ask!

5

HAMSTER CHOW

I reach into the pool and grab Hamstigator.

I pull out a towel, dry him off and put him in

my backpack. I zip it up, sling it over my

shoulder, head downstairs and run across the

street to Brent's house. Brent has an older

sister named Brooke. She's in middle school

with Zack, but more importantly, she has

hamsters. I bet I can borrow some of their food. I knock on the door and after a minute or so, Brent answers.

"Hey Brent. Is your sister home?" I ask, still a little out of breath from running across the street.

"No. She's out with friends," Brent says. "What's up?"

"Well, Hamstigator needs food and I know she has hamsters. Can I borrow some of their food?"

"Who needs food?" Brent asks, confused.

"Hamstigator," I say, as I pull my backpack off my shoulder. I place it at Brent's feet, unzip the top zipper only two inches, and Hamstigator's head pops out.

"Holy cow!" Brent shouts, as he points to the backpack. "You caught a sewer creature!"

"No, this is my new pet! He's half alligator, half hamster. He's a Hamstigator," I say with pride.

"Wow," Brent says, and bends down to get a closer look. "He's cool!"

Brent jumps up and runs out of the room. I hear him talk on the phone to someone, hang up the phone, pick it up again and start talking to someone else. After a few minutes there is a knock on the door. Brent runs to the front door and the next thing I know, five kids from the neighborhood are running inside to check out my new pet. I know all five. They're all in the same third grade class with Brent and me.

Hamstigator still has his head stuck out of the backpack, and all the kids approach him slowly.

"It looks like one of those sewer creatures," Tristan says, as he takes a step toward the backpack. Tristan lives just down the street on Brent's side.

Brayden, who lives 2 houses up on my side of the street, takes a step forward, reaches out and touches the fur on top of Hamstigator's head. Hamstigator tilts his head to the side like a dog and lets Brayden rub behind his ears. Then all the kids come up and start touching Hamstigator.

"This is the coolest thing I've ever seen," says Sydney. She lives right next door to Brent.

"Yeah, he's awesome," I say. "But, he's hungry and I have NO idea what to feed him."

I turn towards Brent as all the kids are still marveling at the coolest pet they've ever seen.

"Can I give him some of the food Brooke feeds her hamsters?" I ask.

"I guess," Brent says. "Let's go check out what she has."

I grab the backpack and all 6 of us follow Brent up the stairs. We reach the top where they have a loft that looks down into the living room. Brooke doesn't keep the hamsters in her room. Instead, their tank is on a table in the loft.

"Here's what they eat," Brent says, handing me a bag of what looks like trail mix.

"This is it?" I ask, looking at the multi-colored flakes, seeds and nuts inside the bag.

The five neighborhood kids look at the bag

of hamster food and at the same time say,

"Eeeeewwww!"

Hamstigator starts scratching at the inside

of the backpack as he eyes the food in my

hand.

Riley, who lives just around the corner from Brent and me, unzips the backpack a little more to get a better look, and Hamstigator leaps out and lands on the floor. He runs a few feet away and freezes. He looks surprised to be free. All of us freeze also, and stare at Hamstigator, waiting to see what he'll do next. All of a sudden, he takes off! He runs out of the room and we all take off after him. He runs down the hall and darts into Brooke's room. All seven of us follow him into the room and shut the door, trapping Hamstigator inside.

"We're not supposed to be in here," Brent says, worried. "My sister will kill me!"

We all spread out as Hamstigator runs around the room exploring every corner he can find. He's fast! And, he can climb! He runs up and down shelves, across the flowery bed, and then up a pink chest of drawers. Everywhere he goes he knocks stuff onto the floor. Each time he passes one of us, we reach for him, but by the time we get close, he's gone. Hamstigator jumps up on Brooke's desk and runs along the top, knocking everything off. He runs into the closet, darting around, up and down the shelves. Clothes, shoes and toys start tumbling out the door.

"Trap him in there," I say, as we all surround the closet in a semi-circle.

Hamstigator climbs up on the top shelf of the closet and turns to look at all of us. Sensing he is cornered, he backs up and takes a huge leap, flying over our heads.

We all watch as he sails through the air above us, and lands on Brooke's bed. He turns to face us and we all freeze. Hamstigator then flashes his 80 teeth, squats down and pees right on Brooke's bed.

"Eeeeeewwwww!" everyone says at the same time. Everyone except Brent. He just buries his head in his hands.

"Brooke is going to kill me!" he says.

I dive forward and scoop Hamstigator up before he can take off again.

"I got ya!" I say, as I wrap both my hands around him. We all walk back to the loft, and I gently place Hamstigator inside the backpack and zip it closed.

I turn to Brent, who still has a look of shock on his face.

"Sorry Brent," I say.

Brent just stares blankly forward. Probably wondering exactly how many hours he has left to live before Brooke comes home.

I grab the bag of hamster food and take off down the stairs.

"Bye you guys," I yell on my way out the door. "See you in school!"

I run across the street, through our front door, up the stairs into my room and over to Hamstigator's tank. I unzip the backpack, grab Hamstigator and place him back in his cage. He runs over to the entrance to the tubes and starts climbing. I open the bag of food and immediately I'm hit with a nasty odor. Yuck! This is what hamsters eat? Gross. I reach inside the tank, grab his food bowl, and fill it with the disgusting mix. As I place the bowl back inside the tank, Hamstigator comes darting out of the tubes and runs over to the bowl.

Hamstigator dives his face into the bowl, but comes up empty. He sniffs around the bowl, but isn't eating. He seems confused at the food and looks up at me.

"It's food," I say. "Hamster food. It looks good," I lie.

Hamstigator turns back to the food, gives it one final sniff and walks away. He comes over to the glass and looks at me with big, sad eyes.

"Sorry buddy," I say. "I really thought that's what you wanted."

Hamstigator slowly walks back over to his pool and lowers himself under the water. I just walk away, scratching my head, not sure what to try next.

6

TURTLES BEWARE

Later, as I'm still trying to figure out what I can feed Hamstigator, I decide to let him take another turn inside his plastic ball. Maybe it will take his mind off being hungry. I stick my hand inside the tank, grab Hamstigator and place him inside the ball. He immediately starts rolling around the room and looks like he's having a good time again, bumping into walls with that same loud thud, changing directions and bumping into more walls.

I realize that I accidentally left my door open just a crack, and the next thing I know, Hamstigator is rolling out the door and down the hallway.

"Hey, come back here, little buddy!" I yell as I run out the door after him.

Zack hadn't shut his door either. Hamstigator rolls right through the opening and into my brother's room. He goes past the bed and heads right for the turtle tank. The turtles are doing what turtles typically do – nothing. Hamstigator speeds up and rams right into the base of their tank.

Both turtles immediately disappear into their shells, which is the only thing turtles ever do quickly.

Hamstigator backs up and plows into the base once again, this time rocking the tank from side to side. One of the turtles is sitting up on a log and falls upside down onto its shell. The other turtle hisses. The tank teeters back and forth as Hamstigator backs up for another ramming shot. Just before he hits it a third time, I reach down and grab his ball.

"Not so fast, Hamstigator," I say. "I don't like those turtles any more than you do, but

Zack will kill me if something happens to them."

Hamstigator stares back at me through that plastic bubble and flashes a mouthful of sharp teeth. If I didn't know any better, I'd swear I saw a devilish smile.

"Let's get you out of that ball before you break something," I say.

I carry Hamstigator into the bathroom and close the door behind me. After that turtle incident, I think he might need to relax a bit. Nothing calms Hamstigator down more than a good old-fashioned bath. I turn on the water and shove the rubber stopper in the drain to let the tub fill up. Once the water gets a couple inches deep, I turn off the faucet and grab Hamstigator's ball. I crack it open and he falls into the tub with a splash. He swims around, ducking under the water a few times and looking like he's having a good time.

I remember that he likes swimming with the

old rubber ducky I played with when I was a

kid.

"Don't go anywhere, Hamstigator. I'll be right back," I say, as I run out of the bathroom.

I zip down the hallway, grab the duck from my bedroom and run back to the bathroom. From the doorway, I toss the duck into the bathtub. It makes a soft squeak as it hits the bottom. No splash?

I walk over and look inside. All the water in the tub is gone, the stopper in the drain is pulled out, and Hamstigator is nowhere to be found. I look around the bathroom, searching for some clue as to where he might be. I check inside all the cabinets, open all the drawers and even look inside the closet. Nothing. Hamstigator has completely disappeared!

7

SURPRISE!

All I can do is stare at the empty bathtub. I have no idea what to do next. All of a sudden, from downstairs, comes a blood-curdling scream.

"Coby Jonathan!" Mom yells. "Get down here!"

Uh oh. You know it can't be good when she uses my middle name.

I race down the stairs, 2 steps at a time. I sprint down the hallway and since I only have socks on my feet, I slide the last 10 feet into the kitchen. I love hardwood floors!

Mom is standing on a chair in front of the sink. She's swinging a broom with both hands over her head like a ninja swings a sword.

"What?" I say, out of breath.

"Get that thing outta my sink!" she yells.

I peek over the edge of the sink and to my

utter surprise, I see Hamstigator's head

sticking out of the drain. All I can see are his eyes, ears, long nose and teeth. He looks like a wet, green Whack-a-Mole. I carefully reach into the sink, but as soon as Hamstigator sees me, he disappears back down the drain. I look up at Mom, who saw the same thing I did. Her face is as red as a tomato. Through gritted teeth, she very slowly says three words that send a shiver down my spine, "Go. Find. Him."

I can't be sure, but I think Mom's mad.

I race out of the kitchen, but I have no idea where I'm going or what I should do next. I hear bangs and pops coming from inside the walls and I freeze in the living room. I stay as quiet as possible, listening to where the noises are coming from.

"Bam!" The hallway!

I run out of the living room, down the hallway to the bottom of the staircase and freeze again. Everything is quiet. I don't move or even breathe for what seems like an eternity. Suddenly, I hear another scream. It's a long, high-pitched noise that sounds like fingernails dragging across a chalkboard. It's Zack!

I speed down the hall, and this time slide past the bathroom door back into the kitchen. I hate hardwood floors! I scramble my way back to the bathroom and find Zack pinned against the bathtub next to the toilet.

"Sewer creature! Sewer creature!" Zack screams. He's yelling at the toilet with a plunger in one hand, swinging it over his head. He looks like a lumberjack about to chop down a big tree.

"What happened?" I ask, trying to catch my

breath.

"I was about to go to the bathroom…so I

lifted up the lid…and IT was in there!" Zack

squeaks, still pointing toward the toilet, with a look of terror on his face.

I don't bother to ask what he saw. I already know. I look down inside the toilet and see Hamstigator swirling around the bowl, having the time of his life. He looks up at me, reaches his alligator arms onto the side of the bowl, and pops his head above the rim. I slowly reach down to grab him, but at the same time, Zack swings the plunger at the bowl. I jump back out of the way just in time. He barely misses Hamstigator's head and the plunger bounces off the side of the toilet.

Zack was never good at that Whack-a-Mole game.

Hamstigator moves to the other side of the bowl and Zack swings at him again. This time he misses by a mile and hits the back of the toilet. The tank cracks and water starts to drip onto the bathroom floor. Hamstigator keeps moving around the bowl, and Zack keeps swinging. Each time, he misses Hamstigator and puts another crack in the toilet. I try to stop him, but I'm afraid if I get in the way I'll become the mole and Zack will start whacking me. Hamstigator finally stops moving and looks up at me. Zack raises the plunger with both hands over his head for one last blow. As it comes down, Hamstigator disappears down the drain and the plunger strikes the toilet, shattering it into a million pieces.

73

Water is spraying everywhere in the bathroom.

"Did I get him?" Zack asks, out of breath.

"I don't think so," I say. "But you certainly taught that toilet a lesson."

8

FEROCIOUS FLOOD

I run out of the bathroom and again try to follow the noises coming from inside the walls. As Hamstigator travels through the pipes, the sounds are getting louder and scarier. I can hear water running throughout the house.

Everywhere Hamstigator goes, the walls crack, pipes burst, and water starts pouring out. It's like watching an earthquake happen inside our house.

I follow the cracks as Hamstigator goes from room to room.

Eventually, every room in the house has water coming out the door.

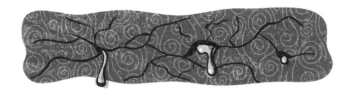

The staircase is now a waterfall. The water runs down the stairs, across the hallway, into the kitchen and down the basement steps.

I watch in horror as the water rises around me. It's only a matter of time before the entire house is going to flood. I splash across the living room, still listening for where Hamstigator is going next.

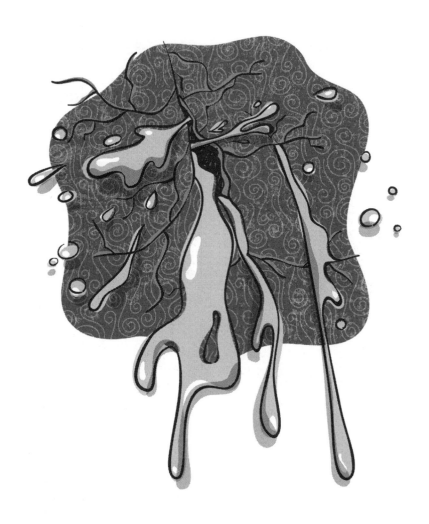

The water in the house is now ankle deep

and still rising. It's even starting to drip onto

my head! I look up, and a huge crack bursts

open above me. A gush of water pours over

my head. I jump out of the way and look up

through the crack. I'm right under Zack's

room.

The falling water carries everything from Zack's room with it. Books, toys, Legos, tennis balls, and other random stuff falls down around me. The water is now up to my knees and still falling from above. Just then, I see Zack's glass aquarium riding the waterfall over the edge and it makes a huge splash right in front of me. It's the turtle tank! I see them, still inside, hissing and darting around as the tank floats towards the front of the house.

I watch it go by, and for the first time since Zack destroyed the toilet, I spot Hamstigator. All I can see are his eyes and the top of his head poking up out of the water. He slowly swims toward the front door, and I finally realize what's going on. Hamstigator is hungry and he's going after the turtles!

I wade through the water in the living room, hoping I can get there before he does. The turtle tank hits the front door, and bobs up and down. The water rises higher and higher around me. I try to move faster through the water, but it's like walking in molasses. Hamstigator speeds up, flashes all his teeth and lunges forward. The turtles, seeing 80 sharp teeth coming at them, quickly disappear into their shells. I dive as Hamstigator comes up out of the water. Just before Hamstigator hits the tank, I catch him in mid air and we both splash down into the water.

"I got you!" I say, as we come up for air.

Just then, the doorbell rings, followed by an angry knock.

"I know you're in there!" The voice sounds very familiar. It's Brooke!

"You and your Hamstigator are dead meat!" Brooke yells. "You owe me a new bed! I'm coming in!"

Hamstigator freezes in my hands as we both turn toward the door. I see the doorknob start to turn.

"Noooo!" I yell. But, it's too late.

The front door flies open, and all the water that had built up behind it rushes out in a huge tidal wave.

It carries the turtle tank, Hamstigator, Brooke and me out into the front yard. Mrs. Cordell, who is walking her dog, Tramp, along the sidewalk, is hit with a huge wave of water that knocks them both out into the street. Hamstigator and I come to rest on the grass at the end of our front yard. We're both drenched and dazed. I'm still holding him in my lap with both hands. Brooke sits up next to me, soaking wet and even madder than she was before. Tramp stands up, shakes off the water, looks over at Hamstigator and immediately starts barking. Mrs. Cordell looks up at the house, looks down at me, points at Hamstigator and yells, "Sewer Creature!"

I just roll my eyes and turn back toward our house.

The front door is broken, windows are cracked, and water continues to pour out into the neighborhood.

I try to fight it, but water starts to pour from my own eyes as well. What will Mom say? What will the neighborhood kids say? What does a new bed cost?

9

DRY AS A BONE

I blink away my tears, close my eyes and hope everything will just go away. At that moment, the sound of running water stops. The feeling of wet clothes on my body is gone, and even Tramp's barking has quieted. I slowly open my eyes, and there I am, still lying in my bed, hands behind my head. My drawing of Hamstigator still hung up on the

wall.

I pull the covers back and look down at the

socks on my feet. Dry as a bone!

I hop out of bed and walk out into the hallway. I see no water on the floors and no cracks on the walls. I go past Zack's room and the dry hardwood cracks and pops under my feet. I love hardwood floors! From inside Zack's room, I hear the faint sound of two turtles as they rustle around their tank. I walk down the stairs and slowly peek into the hallway bathroom. The toilet is still there, and no water is spraying onto the floor. I continue down the hall and into the kitchen. Mom is already there, fixing breakfast and doing first thing in the morning stuff.

"Good morning, Coby," Mom says in a cheery voice.

"Morning Mom," I say.

"You don't still want an alligator for a pet, do you?" Mom asks as she races by.

I think about the question as I wait for her to come back into the room.

"Nah, that was a silly idea," I say. "But, I bet I can come up with something better."

Mom stops and looks over at me. With hands on her hips, she raises one eyebrow and squints in the morning light.

I look at Mom, Mom stares at me, Zack rolls over in his bed, and somewhere in the house, one of the North American Box turtles flips over onto its shell.

THE END

Check out the first Petimals book, Dogopotamus!
Available on Amazon.com.

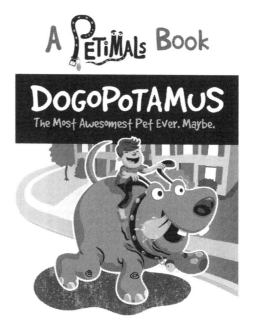

MICHAEL Andrew Fox
Illustrated by Ed Shems

Coby wants a pet. And not just any pet; he wants a hippopotamus. But, apparently you can't have a hippo for a pet, so Coby combines all the things he loves about dogs and all the things he loves about hippos and creates his own NEW pet.

Dogopotamus: The mind of a dog, and the weight of a house means disaster might be just around the corner.

Available NOW at:

BarnesAndNoble.com　　*Amazon.com*　　*TatteredCover.com*

Coming soon...

ELEPHITTEN!

Draw a picture of what you think Elephitten might look like, take a picture and send it to us. You might end up on Petimals.com!

Send your photo to: pics@petimalsbooks.com or post it on facebook.com/petimals

ABOUT THE AUTHOR

Michael Andrew Fox is an Emmy Award winning television producer and author. Inspired by his own two boys, Michael rekindled his passion for writing with his NEW children's book series, Petimals. Hamstigator is his second book.

Michael lives in Colorado with his wife, Eileen and two boys, Zack and Coby.

Visit his website: **www.petimalsbooks.com**

ABOUT THE ILLUSTRATOR

Ed Shems has been illustrating and designing since 1991. Since graduating from the Rhode Island School of Design, Ed has illustrated more than 25 children's books and is currently writing and illustrating his own stories.

Visit his website: **www.edfredned.com**

Made in the USA
San Bernardino, CA
10 August 2017